Geraldine Green

Written by: Blondelia Morris

Illustrated by: Barry Davian

Copyright © 2022 by Blondelia Morris

All rights reserved, including the right to reproduction in whole or in part in any form without written permission except in the case of brief quotations embodied in critical articles or reviews.

Library of Congress Control Number: 2022910373

Geraldine Green

Written by: Blondelia Morris

Illustrated by: Barry Davian

The roll was called in school.

The class sat still as last.

Over the intercom was a voice.

Is Geraldine Green in class?

"Here I am, here I am," she said waving her hand!

"It's me teacher, me teacher," she said taking a proud stand, "my name is Geraldine Green!"

"Come to the office please," the voice over the intercom replied. "Make no stops in between little Miss Geraldine Green," the voice said. Geraldine Green hopped up, rushing out right away.

Her first stop was the lockers giving all 25 locks a twirl.

Then she checked the trophies case, being such an inquisitive little girl.

Outside the window was a little squirrel, running from the ground to a tree.

This caught Geraldine's attention; he was as frisky as he could be.

Next, stop was for water.

Then she looked in every class.

She looked behind every open door.

And she admired her reflection on the shiny floor.

Time is passing, ten minutes to get from here to there. She jumped about and sat in the Security Guard's chair.

The intercom sounded again, "Is Geraldine Green in class?"

She strolled into the office, as if she had just left class. She smiled at the principal and waved her hall pass. "My name is Geraldine Green, I heard you call my name," she said aloud.

"Come in Miss, you are tardy," the principal replied.

"I was playing a game," Geraldine Green started to explain.

The Principal seemed to be surprised.

"What was that strange look in her eyes," thought Geraldine Green?

"Well, I can't believe my eyes," the principal said with great surprise!

"Two girls name Geraldine Green!"

"I have never seen two little girls, with the same name before," she said looking at both girls.

They were a lovely sight to see; two little girls name Geraldine Green!

They hopped, skipped, and twirled about.

Giggling, smiling, and holding hands

these two will always be friends!

You would have cherished it, so

nicely dressed and so clean.

Two little girls name Geraldine Green!

The intercom boomed again, "The Green girls are on their way!" "They just left my office; they really made my day!"

Author Blondelia Morris

Blondelia Morris was born in Greenville, North Carolina on April 12, 1925 and raised in Norfolk, Virginia. She attended John T. West Elementary and Booker T. Washington High School in Norfolk, I.C. Norcom High School in Portsmouth, Virginia. Due to hardships she dropped out of school in the 11th grade and joined the work force. In 1958, she volunteered in her neighborhood school for two years. Where she applied for a job as a paraprofessional and realized that a high school diploma was necessary. She immediately returned to school and earned a GED. This enabled her to become gainfully employed as a paraprofessional and later a secretary with Norfolk City Schools.

Continuing to study she completed required courses from the Institute of Children's Literature in 1992 and Writers Digest School in Ohio, in 1993. With an accumulation of classes and further studies, she received a Masters in Drama and Directing in 2002 from Northwestern University. Despite, Blondelia Morris hearing loss and vision impairment she continues to share, write, and create. She has written several books like Hag – A- Ma- Doodle, poems and plays. Working with children fostered a love for writing that she enjoys today, at the present and marvellous age of 97!